DOUBLE JACK

Book 1 in the series,
THE CRIME FILES OF KATY GREEN

DOUBLE JACK

Book 1 in the series,
THE CRIME FILES OF KATY GREEN

by Gene O'Neill

with illustrations
by Greg Chapman

and series introduction
by John Palisano

DARK MOON BOOKS
Los Angeles, California

Interior layout by Eric J. Guignard
Cover design by Eric J. Guignard
www.ericjguignard.com

Front cover illustration by Jelena Mišljenović
www.instagram.com/jelena.misljenovic

Interior illustrations by Greg Chapman
https://darkartiste.wordpress.com

First Dark Moon Books edition published in October, 2017
Library of Congress Control Number: 2017951691
ISBN-13: 978-0-9988275-6-8 (paperback)
ISBN-13: 978-0-9988275-7-5 (e-book)

DARK MOON BOOKS
Los Angeles, California
www.DarkMoonBooks.com

Made in the United States of America

This book is dedicated to:
Mu Chuisle

CHAPTERS

"The so-called experts agree that serial killers always have at least three common events in their early childhoods: torturing small animals, lighting fires, and wetting their beds. A complete crock of bull pucky, cuz I never wet the bed."

—*John A. Malenko, jailhouse interview.*

MEETING KATY GREEN: AN INTRODUCTION TO GENE O'NEILL'S *THE CRIME FILES OF KATY GREEN*

BY JOHN PALISANO

I n the beginning, something goes wrong: A great detective commences with the problem and does their best to find where it started so they can steer it toward a conclusion.

So it is that we find ourselves, as with most great mysteries, right smack dab in the middle of this first book's problem, experiencing a visceral sex crime. Immediately, we're rattled and upset.

Cut to Katy Green, a young detective. In a twist of meta callback, she's working on a novel about an Indigo Man, based on a famous story of hers that appeared in *Twilight Zone* magazine. This is a nod to the author's own *Cal Wild* chronicles, especially *The Burden of Indigo*, which have all recently been reprinted. But is Katy Green a surrogate character for Gene O'Neill? Is she a female wish-fulfillment? No. She's something else entirely. Even with the Easter egg nods to others of the author's work sprinkled throughout the series, Katy Green's ultimate connection to Gene's work is in her being a fully realized, strong, and smart female character, equal and effective as the men, if not more so.

As the sex crimes and murders add up, Katy and her partner Johnny are faced with how these crimes are affecting them personally.

This is another hallmark of O'Neill's storytelling: the darkest events have repercussions. They aren't included simply for a thrill, they change people. They make people act differently and, in this case, think outside their comfort zones.

It would be easy to dismiss a mystery thriller if you only hear or read a synopsis. Since the 1970s, there have been many serial killers in the Bay Area such as the Trailside Killer and the Zebra Killers. This has certainly been an area that's been covered many times. There have been several particularly notorious cases in the Bay Area, but none more explosive and explored than the Zodiac Killer.

There are echoes of these instances in this series, especially the sex-fuelled crimes of the Zodiac Killer. Although, in a terrific twist, and one I don't want to give away, O'Neill dashes expectations of assumptions and cliché.

Katy Green often finds inspirations and clues to the motivations and identification of the perpetrators in odd common places and events of her own. Although many detective stories often have their intrepid thinkers seemingly solving crimes through deductive reasoning, Katy Green uses some unique experiences of being a young woman to her advantage. This aspect adds a very intriguing color to the proceedings.

This is the thrust of the serial killer in the aptly named *Double Jack*, the first book of three in *The Crime Files of Katy Green* series.

Often, women are seen as vulnerable, and stronger-imagined men come to the rescue at the last minute. That sort of *deus ex machina* doesn't need to happen for Katy Green. She's a fully-realized and extremely capable detective in her own right.

Of course, she *is* nuanced. There are mistakes. She's very much a human being. There are often errors, though, where she learns about herself and is able to refine a process, or to dial down a hypothesis. She's a fascinating character to travel with, for sure. I wondered how these stories came to be…

So, to sate my curiosity, I asked the author, and wanted to share herein an excerpt of his response, which helps illuminate not only origin of the character, but also Gene's own writing influence.

"All three books were written some years ago, so they are early work. I think as you mention they all contain elements perhaps more pronounced in my more recent work. The two longer novels actually contain a strong dark fantasy element. One other maybe interesting note: When I was the Vice-President for operations in an insulation plant, our welders all came out of the San Quentin welding program. One morning, a young welder didn't come to work. I asked the welding boss, 'What happened?' He said the welder's parole was revoked. He was the Good Samaritan Rapist. Went back down for a long time at nineteen. That was the idea for *Double Jack*. True story."

Gene's known mostly as a science fiction and horror writer, having received many accolades in both. I wondered where the detective stories originated with him, and Gene told me the following.

"Early on as a reader, I admired detective/mystery stories. I still like to read mystery and thrillers, the work of Connelly, Sanford, and Deaver are three favorites. So, I think it was natural that I would try my hand at this type of story. The novels were first published as limited edition/deluxe edition hardbacks by Bad Moon Books. The novella was a limited edition trade paperback by a small press now out of business."

And was there a real-life inspiration for Katy Green?

Gene revealed to me: "My daughter is named Kaydee, and is a tough, strong woman. Katy Green is modeled on her, the real Kaydee."

That's pretty darn cool, and speaks highly of Gene as a father.

When I first met Gene O'Neill many years back, I was impressed with his very diverse resume. Not only had he gone to Clarion, but Gene had lived a varied and extraordinary life. In addition to the several different jobs he told me he'd held, he'd also had a career as a champion boxer. He even showed me the twisted fingers to prove it. For me? It was impossible to separate the man from most of his stories. There's an authenticity to his scenes and the fights in his tales of San Francisco's beautiful and tough-as-diamonds Tenderloin district. Very often, he'll tell a story of someone inhabiting these seemingly dark, forbidding places, and will reveal a hidden world adjacent to the hustle and bustle of the working class city folk.

It's this slow unraveling that works in concert with *The Crime Files of Katy Green* series, as well. Something that appears rather straightforward soon shows signs of something else peeking through... something supernatural... something unexplained... something that should not be there. As the *Katy Green* series continues into its second book, we are introduced to a much larger canvas, and a much more formidable foe in *Shadow of the Dark Angel*. Then, *Deathflash* the third book, brings even more to the table, transcending the tropes and expectations of a classic detective series, while still satisfying and remaining true to that same time-honored formula.

When Eric J. Guignard asked me to write an introduction to this series, I immediately said yes. Gene served as a mentor to me in the Horror Writers Association, and it was through his tough, smart feedback that I produced my first pro-level writing, which led to my first pro-level sales. During that time, I feel I also made a damn good friend. Gene's passion is infectious. At conventions, he's known to use his signing slots to read a little from his own work, but then using the remainder of the time championing and featuring other upcoming writers he's helping out.

And like Katy Green, and like so many characters in Gene's work, when he's got your back, he's *got your back*. A favorite story of mine took place a few years ago when Gene and Gord Rollo visited Los Angeles. We took a car full of writers in my old Camry through a personal sightseeing drive through the city. We ended up looking over the city, high on top of Mulholland Drive, taking in the same view as so many of those great old Los Angeles private eyes.

Later, we all ended up at the pool at Gene's hotel, doing what writers do when they get together: talking, hanging out, swimming into the late hours. Naturally, as the hours grew late, one of the guests above the pool complained about the noise. A hotel employee came out and told us we had to leave; it wasn't the fact that maybe we *were* in the wrong, but that the employee decided to yell unnecessarily at us in a thoroughly condescending manner. Well, Gene wasn't having it. He handed this guy his ass on a platter. After all, Gene was a guest, too, and he'd paid his money, and he'd be damned if we'd have the pool time cut short. The guy backed down and slunk away into the shadows. Gord celebrated the victory by doing a somersault, feet over head, right into the pool. Gene sat back down on the lounger and watched over his flock, arms folded. Gene didn't swim, but he sure as hell made sure we could. Me? I was just damn thankful I was on Gene's team that night instead of the hotel's.

It's that same kind of charisma, power, and chutzpah one feels when reading Gene's stories: even with the craziest, scariest stuff going on, you always feel that Gene is going to guide you through to the other side, relatively intact. Readers will get that when knee-deep into *The Detective Files of Katy Green*, too.

This trio—a novella and two full-length novels—was originally published individually as one-time, extremely limited releases. Finally, they are available widely, in the author's preferred versions, with spot illustrations by Greg Chapman.

I hope you enjoy this series as much as I have.

Welcome to the mind and world of Gene O'Neill through Katy Green.

—John Palisano
September 7, 2017

THUY NGUYEN

CRIME SCENE NOTES

Name: Thuy Nguyen

Ethnicity/ Gender: Vietnamese-American Female

Age: 25 years old

Family: Single parent of 2-year-old girl

Occupation: Computer Programmer

Trauma: Sexually Assaulted, Head and Facial Trauma, Cracked Ribs, Strangled, Hyoid Bone Fractured

1

*T*hump, thump, thump.

At first Thuy thought she'd missed seeing something in her lane because of the heavy downpour of rain, and ran right over it. She braked, slowing the Escort, but the strange racket continued, coming from somewhere at the back of her car.

Thump, thump, thump.

Then she knew... A flat tire!

Oh, no, she thought, clenching her teeth. She was already late picking up Sarah from Grandmother Anh, delayed almost an hour because of the late meeting of her MIS section with a consultant from IBM at General Services Headquarters, the State office located in downtown Sacramento.

Now this.

Grandmother always went to bed early, usually around 7:00. Glancing in her mirrors, she signaled and carefully pulled over onto the shoulder of the inside lane on Interstate-5 heading northwest out of the city toward the airport. Thuy activated the emergency flashers. She would've been home to her duplex apartment in Natomas in about five minutes even with the traffic slowed down by the rain if it hadn't been for this problem.

Thuy just sat and looked out the windshield at the blurry headlights coming from the other direction on the freeway. It was truly pouring out there, the raindrops making a steady *plunking* sound on the roof above her... And she'd never changed a tire before—didn't really know how to begin. She took her cell phone out of her purse—

It was dead.

"Oh, no," she said in exasperation. It was definitely her unlucky day. Her Vietnamese grandmother probably could've helped prevent all this if Thuy had just listened to her admonitions earlier this morning, when she dropped off Sarah over at Grandmother's half of the duplex. But she'd been in too big of a hurry, even skipping breakfast. Grandmother had said there were bad portents, including the day's date, an early morning barking dog disturbing a lucky dream, and Channel 10's weather prediction of an unexpected bad storm sweeping in from the Pacific. She'd been right of course. Thuy should've listened, taken the extra time to observe the old way to ward off bad luck—pray, burn some incense, and place a little fruit and candy on the ancestral alter in Grandmother's bedroom. But no! She ignored the warning. Too big of a hurry. Rush, rush, rush all day long. Now *this*.

She just sat for another minute and looked with a sense of helplessness out the windshield, the heavy downpour of thumbnail-size raindrops splattering against the green hood of the little Ford.

And that's when the pickup with the green and blue CalTrans logo on its door pulled over close, slowing almost to a stop, checking the situation out, and then pulling up to park on the shoulder up in front of her car.

Maybe her luck was changing, Thuy thought, as a huge, white guy with a short pony-tail stepped out of the pickup and came around to the passenger side of the Escort. He gestured and she rolled down the window.

The big man smiled warmly and stuck his head in out of the rain. "Howdy, ma'am, can I help y'all?" he said in a soft, vaguely southern drawl.

"Oh, the ancestors have indeed tilted their heads my way," Thuy mouthed gratefully under her breath. Then, aloud to the stranger:"I think I've got a flat, sir, the rear left tire."

"You do indeed, I guarantee you on that," the CalTrans man said, nodding and gesturing back with his thumb without looking at the tire. "Noticed it when I saw your flashers and came up on y'all. Pop the trunk, and I'll get out your spare and jack, and switch tires. Take just a minute."

"Oh, would you?" Thuy said, popping the trunk latch. "That would be wonderful, but you're going to get yourself completely soaked working out there." She began to crack her door to get out and help him.

"No sweat, ma'am," the CalTrans man said, reaching in and lightly restraining her right shoulder. "You stay in there and keep dry. No sense in both of us getting wet." He went around to the back and disappeared when he lifted the trunk wide open. Then he was back in view and ducking down at her left rear tire, the steady stream of cars zooming by and splashing water apparently not bothering him.

The rain also seemed to cooperate at that moment by reducing from a downpour to just a heavy drizzle.

In only a couple of minutes the CalTrans man was tossing in the flat tire and tools, dropping down the trunk lid... And then he was poking his wet, grinning face back in the window of Thuy's car.

"Got 'er done, ma'am."

"Oh, how can I thank you enough," she said, reaching over and shaking his extended wet hand.

His huge hand tightened roughly on hers, squeezing and hurting her. "Oh, we'll figure out a way, I bet you on that." He nodded, the warm smile slowly thinning out, his expression actually hardening, and his gaze appearing almost... lascivious. "Maybe we can go get a cup of coffee or something, get warmed up, become better acquainted, you know."

And that's when Thuy became suspicious. For the first time she noticed the man wasn't wearing the characteristic CalTrans neon-orange vest or even a nametag ID—he was dressed in washed but stained whites, like a house painter. And he no longer looked the least bit friendly either—almost menacing, in fact. Alarms bells were blasting off in her head now. She wasn't going any place with this stranger. She tried to jerk her hand free. But he only tightened his trap-like grip.

"Let go!" Thuy said in a shaky voice. "Please."

He only clenched tighter.

Frightened badly now, Thuy tried to scratch the huge man, deeply raking the inside of his wrist with the fingernails of her free hand.

"*Ouch.*"

Still hanging on tightly, he punched her squarely in the face with his free hand, making her eyes water as she gasped in a deep breath, her whole face exploding with pain, and her nose beginning to trickle blood onto her white blouse.

Terrified now, Thuy tried to blink away the tears while attempting to wriggle free. Which only caused the big man to almost jerk her arm out of its shoulder socket. "Quit it, bitch!"

At that moment, Thuy knew she was in serious trouble... And for a fraction of a moment she clearly saw little Sarah's smiling face, the two-year-old waving goodbye—

"Get in the back seat, girl!" the huge man ordered, all good humor gone from his voice and mean, penetrating dark eyes.

He held her hand in his clamp-like grip through the window, then carefully cracked the door and let go a moment, before pulling her roughly out of the driver's seat and out into the drizzle... Then, she felt herself being dragged around, and tossed roughly into the back of the Escort. The scary big guy moved quickly over her, pinning her down with his great bulk and almost crushing the air out of her with his upper body; then he was pushing up, flipping her skirt up in her face, and roughly ripping away her panties with one hand while keeping her firmly pressed down with the other.

Oh, no, this can't be happening to me right out here in the open, Thuy thought, trying desperately to twist her leg and shield herself.

But it was.

2

Gook poontang! Jack thought with a surge of elation, after he pulled up next to the stranded car with the flashing emergency light and flat tire, and glanced in at the petit, cute Asian driver. Man, it was definitely his lucky day! He eased around and parked in front of the disabled '94 Escort.

Oh, how he dearly loved these little-bitty gals with big bushes. He'd been smitten with a bar girl in Japan when he was eighteen, way back during his first cruise to the Far East in '87 while stationed on the aircraft carrier, USS Ranger. And over his Navy years, he regularly fell in lust in the red light districts of Subic Bay, Hong Kong, Yokohama, Bangkok, and Naha. He winced slightly, remembering the bad episode on Okinawa just over two years ago, when he'd got a little too rough with a skinny-ass broad in The Body Shop juke joint near White Beach. Ended up having to drag her outside, down an alley, and take some without paying. During the process he broke her jaw and beat her up pretty badly, which had almost cost him some serious brig time after the Shore Patrol caught up with him. But he'd lucked out of that tight spot, not even court-martialed—no witnesses, the prostitute herself refusing to press charges. Only to get denied re-enlistment early last year because of his weight: *Over optimal weight for an enlisted sailor.*

That's what they said in his paperwork, but he knew it was really all about his numerous public scuffles over pussy being brought to command attention—he'd had three Captain's Masses, even once lost some stripes in a Summary Court-Martial.

Smiling wryly, he had to admit his weight *had* gotten a little out of control, steadily rising over 300 pounds during his last year in the Navy—and even more so lately. But not really all so bad back then for a guy over six-three—he was just a husky sailor, he rationalized.

Jack set the brake on his recently purchased pickup. Actually he'd almost stolen it at a CalTrans auction a week or so ago, but hadn't had time to sand and paint over the logo yet, still using his old '79 Courier pickup for most of his commercial painting jobs.

Anyhow, even after all this time he still couldn't come to terms with the Navy brass booting him out after *twelve* fucking years of patriotic service—but a good discharge at least, nothing too bad on his record. *Ha*, the dumb fucks may've been concerned with his minor dustups, but they never even suspected he was involved with those two major fuck-ups in the Philippines and Hong Kong. As he climbed out of the front seat, he thought about the broads he'd had to permanently put down to keep quiet—the memory of over-the-top rough sex making him semi-hard as he slipped away from his new wheels.

He put on his charmer grin as he motioned for the woman to roll down her window. He'd fix this little flat, take her grateful ass somewhere not quite so public, a rest stop maybe, and then at leisure, he'd check out that glorious big bush… *Oh, man, some spiced huggings later tonight.* He licked his lips in anticipation, the wicked thoughts only widening his grin.

But after fixing her tire, the bitch wanted to fight him instead of cooperating. She scratched his wrist, even drawing blood. *God damn it!* Jack got mad. He punched her in the nose just hard enough to get her attention, or so he thought… But even that didn't do the job. No way. She was a scrappy little shit, all right.

Well, it wasn't going to do her any good, he thought, ordering: "Get in the back seat, girl!"

He was going to take some of that bushy pussy right out here on the freeway whether she cooperated or not. Her frantic struggles only aroused him more.

He was finished, sweating heavily, just laying still on the girl, trying to catch his breath. The little wildcat wasn't making any noise now at all, not even that funny gurgling shit she'd been doing just a minute or two ago.

Jack pushed up off of her and looked down.

Man, the bitch looked fucked-up, *big time*. Squashed kinda flat under his weight, like all the air was crushed out of her. Nose bleeding pretty bad now. Neck all scraped up, bruised, and twisted at a funny angle. No, she wasn't looking too good. Jack realized he'd gone a little too far again, just like those other two whores overseas a couple years ago. This one was going to stay down permanently, too, *I bet you on that—*

Well, *fuck* the little shit, he thought, backing out of the car into the rain, quickly pulling up his pants and tucking in his painter's white shirt. Serves the stupid bitch right for being so fucking ungrateful. Damn, it was pouring heavily again. He shivered and glanced furtively at the lights zooming by in the rainy darkness, nobody paying close attention to him, he hoped.

Nah, they were all in too big a hurry to get home for supper and out of this rainstorm.

"Good deal, Lucille!" he said, and then thought, I'll just haul my ass out of here, leave the gook snatch right there in the back seat. Be a nice surprise for some fucking CHP.

He chuckled dryly.

Then, Jack slipped into his newly purchased State-used pickup and drove off into the rainy night, not giving the battered and dead young woman another thought.

3

It was late, only a few minutes before midnight, and Katy Green was at her desk iMac in her townhouse near Sac State, working thoughtfully on the three-page-outline for her first novel, *The Indigo Man*.

The phone rang. *Oh-no*, not a good sign this time of night, she thought.

"Hello," she said cautiously, after first standing and stretching her 6-foot, athletic frame—she'd once been a basketball star out at Sac State as an undergraduate eight and a half years ago.

"Hey, Katy, hope I didn't wake you up."

It was Harlan Bundy from work. *Really* not a good sign.

"No, I was *just* doing a little writing," she said, unable to keep the cranky sarcasm from her tone.

"Good," Harlan said, the niceties apparently over. "Captain Silver is calling you and Johnny in tomorrow for a 10:00 meeting."

Tomorrow, Tuesday, was her and, her partner, Johnny Cato's scheduled comp day off. She'd planned on finishing the outline and starting the rough draft that she wanted to show an agent at the *BayCon* science fiction convention coming up in six or seven months. Over the past couple years, she'd sold twelve short stories to good mystery, science fiction, and fantasy magazines and anthologies that were pretty well-received, and thought she might be able to do more with her writing—expanding her most famous short story from *The Twilight Zone Magazine* into a full length novel. But her day job as a homicide detective with Sacramento PD was intervening tonight, and obviously tomorrow, too.

"What's up, Harlan?" she asked Bundy.

"Patrick McHugh and my turn in the barrel tonight, as you know. We got called out and covered a bad one over on I-5 that may be right up your alley. Victim's a young mother. Picked up some good stuff out there, but Channel 3 and the *Bee* showed up, and will probably be making a big fuss about this one by tomorrow—victim left a two-year-old daughter. So Long John wants you guys helping us out—full court press on this case. You know the drill."

"What do you mean, up *my* alley?" Katy asked, not trying to hide the lingering trace of resentment in her voice, as she reluctantly turned over the three single-spaced pages of her outline.

"Well, like I said, we got a young mother. She's savagely raped, beat up, and strangled in the back seat of her car—now get this—right in the middle of evening commuter traffic, just off the side of the freeway, hundreds of cars whizzing by within a few feet during the assault. Guy has to be a stone-cold nutter with ice water in his veins, you know, even with the rainstorm kind of covering his ass."

Katy had a growing reputation in the department for having good instincts investigating homicides that looked like the work of obviously sociopathic or even psychotic perps. Usually bizarre murders that quickly stirred the public imagination and subsequent political attention.

"Uh-huh," Katy said, intrigued now by Harlan's brief description, her novel outline temporarily forgotten. "The crime scene has been closed down, I assume. Body already taken in by the ME's people? Nothing left out there to look over, right?"

"Yeah, sorry, Katy. McHugh and I didn't think of calling you right away until we hooked up later with Long John at headquarters. I think the quick media response and interest stirred up his concern. Anyhow, I wanted to give you a head's up. We'll lay out what we have for you and Johnny tomorrow morning. See you then."

"Bye, Harlan."

The next morning the phone rang at 7:00 a.m. jerking Katy up out of a sound sleep. She knew it had to be her partner, John Cato. No matter what time he got home the night before or in whatever condition—which was alcohol- and drug-free currently, since he'd started going to AA and NA meetings two months ago at her insistence—he was always up early and ready to roll.

"Yeah, Johnny," she said in a sleep-hoarse voice. "Top of the morning to you too, partner."

"Check out the paper, kiddo." It was him alright, and she could almost see the frown in his voice and on his face. He was handsome in a rugged way with scarred eyebrows and broken nose—he'd been a two-time California middleweight champion golden gloves boxer as a teenager, and later an undefeated light-heavyweight out at Sac State, before the school eventually cancelled its fight program sometime in the late '60s, finally conforming like most colleges to NCAAP pressure after a series of serious boxing injuries.

"No rest for the wicked, girl," he added, quietly laughing.

She kept the phone to her ear, quickly pulled on a faded-blue kimona from the foot of her bed, and went out her front door.

Shivering slightly on the way back to the kitchen, she unfolded the *Sacramento Bee*, the headline jumping out at her:

GREEN HORNET & CATO ASSIGNED I-5 MURDER

"Okay, I get it," she said, "and am looking over the article, now…"

Since being assigned to homicide four years ago and partnering with John Cato, the pair had solved a string of five pretty high profile cases, and recently—because of their last names—the press and TV had started dubbing them *The Green Hornet & Cato*, even though Johnny's last name didn't quite match up with the original comic book hero's. Katy didn't really care, but Johnny thought it was typical media bullshit, and the notoriety just made their work that much more difficult: Public expecting miracles. Probably true to some degree, she thought. So he apparently found the blaring headline especially galling this morning on their supposed comp day off.

She chuckled. "I'm up, awake now, and getting some coffee, pal," a little more sunshine in her voice. "Looks like we may have an interesting case here."

"Yeah… well, see you later at 10:00 at the office," her partner said, still sounding slightly peeved. Katy knew he'd be over it and straining at the bit to get started by the time of their meeting.

"I'll be there, pal."

Katy Green smiled to herself and read over the article again. The paper was calling the killer: *The Good Samaritan Rapist*. The *Bee* said one of the first on-scene detectives had interviewed a motorist who'd doubled back to the scene to help after spotting the likely perp changing the outside rear tire on the victim's Ford Escort during the heavy downpour. The perp had apparently stopped, voluntarily changed the flat tire for the young woman, Thuy Nguyen, in the rainstorm, *then* proceeded to savagely beat, rape, and finally strangle her to death. Doing all this in maybe ten minutes at most.

Katy set the paper down, already beginning to work the bizarre case in her head, looking absently over at the steaming coffee.

Man, that just didn't compute. Why would he do that, fix a tire out in that downpour last night? she asked herself. If he were only going to rape and kill her afterwards? Was it a spur of the moment decision to rape her and then kill her? Or what? And ten minutes to accomplish all of that? Of course she didn't have any ready answers, but the questions were being neatly filed away in her head to address later.

At 10:00 a.m. Harlan Bundy and Patrick McHugh laid out what they'd come up with last night and earlier this morning to Katy, Johnny, and Captain Silver, who was also sitting in with four of his homicide detectives. For a case like this there seemed to be quite a bit of potentially good evidence left at the scene.

Harlan started first. "Perp left some latent fingerprints all over the Escort, inside and out, most of those outside blurred by the rain though. Also left his DNA, both semen and apparently his skin under her fingernails. The lab has started working on all this right now—top priority designation. Hope we get an early report on the prints by tomorrow at the latest. One witness so far, a passing motorist. He'd spotted the apparent perp changing the flat tire—but really had no physical description, other than he thought the crouched-over guy was *probably* white. And no description of the perp's vehicle either. Witness paid no attention to that, the heavy rain restricting visibility somewhat out there at the time."

"*Bee* and TV must've talked to this witness?" Captain Silver asked in his high-pitched voice, which was at odds with his short, husky build, bald-head, and lined black features—he looked like a middle-aged jock gone to seed. His department nickname, Long John, even more incongruent; of course no one in the whole Sacramento police department called him that to his face.

"Yeah," Harlan replied, frowning. "Of course Patrick and I didn't give them do-diddly, Boss. But in addition to questioning the witness, it looks like they may've picked up a bit more *inside* information somewhere later on with some of the physical details that they published this morning."

Katy suspected the Chief's office or perhaps someone in the forensics lab. She figured Long John would actively check that out—department leaks to the media made his dark features almost red. In fact, he didn't look really cheerful right now.

She shifted her attention back to Bundy and McHugh, the partners sitting side-by-side. The first responding homicide detectives didn't have too much more to add to the meeting. Patrick said that they were trying to get other witnesses to call in, hoping for a description of the perp's vehicle, in addition to whatever else they could come up with. The *Bee* and Channels 3 and 10 were all cooperating by requesting call-ins from witnesses in today's paper and on the noontime TV news programs, and the stations would repeat the requests again early tonight.

Typical early investigation so far of a homicide not immediately offering obvious suspects or early confessions, Katy thought.

There was a lag in the conversation.

"Questions?" Captain Silver asked, looking directly at Johnny and then Katy with raised eyebrows.

She nodded, and said, "Well, yeah. That ten minutes bothers me, you know. Tell us again what the witness said happened during that time period exactly." She looked over at Bundy, who sat nearest to her.

Harlan cleared his throat and explained, "Well, passing by he saw the perp changing the flat, figured he could use some help—"

"Why would he come back to help a stranger in a heavy rainstorm like last night?" Katy asked, more than a trace of skepticism in her voice. "That doesn't seem at all likely to me."

"Maybe *he's* the Good Samaritan," Johnny suggested.

Bundy ignored Johnny's attempt to be funny, and replied, "Patrick actually talked to him first and asked him that *very* question." He turned away from Katy to his partner beside him for clarification.

McHugh sat up straighter, and explained, "Well, Johnny's probably right, you know. The witness said he helped because he felt it was the neighborly right thing to do. Guy is a legit do-gooder. Deacon in his Church of God, ten-year volunteer for meals-on-wheels for seniors, regularly gives blood, and that sort of thing... "

The detective paused, shrugged with a slightly cynical expression on his face, and nodded with raised eyebrows as if saying: *Unbelievable, I know, but true nevertheless.* Then he continued: "Anyway, he doubled back to help, after having to go up the freeway almost two miles to the next exit. No closer over-crossings out there before then. He estimated the time to come back was maybe ten minutes. I doubt he could do it quite that quickly though with poor visibility and all... However long it took, the perp was gone by the time the witness got back. And the victim had been left raped and dead in the back seat. Fortunately, this witness didn't touch anything at the scene, just called it in on his cell. But he hung around and got himself interviewed by both Channel 3 and the *Bee*, like Harlan said." McHugh glanced around the circle of faces for any more specific questions.

There were none, everyone sitting in silence for a few moments.

"Anything else for now?" Long John finally asked, glancing at Katy and Johnny.

They slowly shook their heads.

"Okay, Bundy, you're lead on this one," the Captain said, standing up. "Bring me up to speed each morning at 10:00. Okay?"

"Right, Boss."

Harlan divided up early responsibilities for both detective teams, set a next meeting time for all of them at 9:00 a.m. the next morning. Then, they broke up for everyone to get busy.

As assigned, Katy and Johnny would begin today by checking out the victim's family and friends for potential leads, then later they'd come back downtown to her employer at General Services.

ANGIE JONES

CRIME SCENE NOTES

Name: Angie Jones

Ethnicity/ Gender: African-American Female

Age: 19 years old

Family: Single

Occupation: College student—art major

Trauma: Stabbed 21 times with a shading pencil, Two Cracked Ribs, Nose Broken

---

!

A ngie glanced down at the fuel gauge on her stalled beat-up, old Buick LeSabre.

The needle was pegged way past *EMPTY*.

"Oh, holy crap!" she said, turning the ignition key over once more, a kind of half-hearted and stubborn hope that maybe the gas gauge was just broken, too, like everything else on the damn car. Her brother had given it to her five and a half months ago when he got his new Kawasaki. But she'd had nothing but trouble, already fixing the brakes and replacing first the battery and then an alternator—whatever the heck that was. The most recent repair work a month ago had tapped out most of her last two paychecks from her part-time McDonald's job on Del Paso Boulevard, even after she increased her workload to thirty hours a week. She'd scrimped on putting in any gas today, hoping to make it back to Del Paso Heights after eating lunch with Gertie Mae where her friend worked at the Food Circus near the State Fairgrounds. She would finally get paid again tomorrow afternoon.

But, now, here she was sitting out on I-80 as it rapidly grew dark, right at her turn-off and still three miles from home… Delbert, her twin brother, not answering his cell. She couldn't call her pops at his new job in the Wal-Mart shipping department out in Natomas. He'd be pissed off, for sure. Man, what should she do now? *Hmm…*

She got out after releasing the hood and propped it up. She thought that's what the DMV recommended when stalled out like she was. Maybe a CHP would come along and stop. Man, that'd be a first, she thought wryly, a cop helping rather than hassling her. The local patrol cops out in Del Paso Heights were always stopping her and her friends when they were hanging around in a group after dark at the 7-Eleven or Rec Center. Figured they were either gang-bangers or selling dope. Man, that was a laugh. Her pops would've worn a layer of skin off her raggedy booty. He'd promised Angie's mother, before she died two years ago of colon cancer, that neither Delbert or Angie would ever be gang-bangers or dope dealers. And, indeed, they'd both graduated from high school last year with good grades, were working part time, and attending American River Community College. Delbert was interested in English and History, thought he wanted to teach high school. In addition to her required general courses, she was taking two art classes, hoping to maybe be a commercial or graphic artist someday or maybe an art teacher—

Whoa, looked like her lucky day! Cal Trans guy was stopping and getting out of his pickup. Man, this white dude was some kind of big boy for sure, she thought, almost as huge as that 49ers' tackle with the two basketball playing daughters... ole Bubba Harris. But maybe a little bit out of shape. Yeah, he was a fatty, all right, she thought, as he moved up closer, looking pretty agile for his size.

"Howdy, ma'am, can y'all use a hand?" he asked, real polite-like.

Angie nodded, temporarily switching off her personal radar because of the current emergency. Big boy sounded like he come from Texas or New Orleans, some place weird like that. But other than that, he seemed to be okay, like a good dude.

"Sure can, Big Fella," she said, smiling, real friendly-like herself. "Didn't fill up with gas today. Think I ran out. Kind of dumb, eh?"

He shrugged, still smiling, and pointed to the back of his pickup. "Got an empty gallon can right back there with my painting stuff. Let's go fill it up at a station in Del Paso Heights."

"All right!" Angie said. She followed the guy back to his pickup, and slipped into the front seat.

In his funny drawl the big dude kept up a steady dialogue of sort of dull chatter, until he started talking about a just released movie, *Crash*, that Angie wanted to see, but wouldn't have the bread until her next paycheck. Movie sounded way cool. She'd been so caught up in his description that she hadn't paid real close attention in the last few minutes to where he was driving, *until* he turned off onto the old river road heading *out* of Del Paso Heights toward Marysville.

"Hey, hold on there, Big Fella, we must've passed a pair of service stations open back there. Where you think you're taking me now?" Her personal radar was back on, and blinking a big green blip, almost screaming an accompanying warning: *danger, danger, danger.*

Whoa, dude wasn't grinning or talking anymore... and he looked pretty damn bad-ass, too. Not good. *Uh-uh.*

Angie, slipped her hand into her little purse and wrapped her fingers tightly around a sharpened pencil she always carried for security—one of the large, long, extra-thick ones she used for shading in her drawing class. At the same time, she ordered: "Okay, stop this fucking pickup right now and let me out, fat boy!" She steeled herself, trying to bring her rapid breathing under control.

He braked sharply and pulled off the road, after glancing back over his shoulder.

Man, there were no cars in sight either way now on the river road. And it was definitely getting real dark.

Big dude reached over to grab her… and Angie scooted away back against the door, pulling the sharp pencil out of her purse. As he reached across toward her shoulder, she stabbed out with a poking motion, penetrating the web-like skin on his hand between his thumb and forefinger. Whatever this fat white boy had in mind, it wasn't going to be easy, Angie thought, drawing back and trying to stab the asshole again right in the face.

But the big dude was surprisingly quick, slipping his head slightly to the side like a boxer, easily eluding the thrust of the makeshift weapon, and he followed that up by slamming the heel of his uninjured hand solidly into her throat.

Ugh.

Choking, Angie coughed, gasped for breath, blinked away tears, almost blacking out for a moment. But she sucked in a deep breath, pulled herself quickly together, and attempted to fight back, swinging out wildly with her free fist, but unable to see sharply through the teary blur. She struck him a glancing blow on the side of his forehead.

"You fucking black bitch!" he roared, scooting across into her half of the seat.

Then, the big guy attacked, dipping slightly and jarring her with a shoulder rammed into her chest and knocking the air from her, grabbing her wrist in a vise grip, and yanking the sharp pencil out of her hand with his free hand. Following up, he head-butted her in the face, her nose making a loud *cracking* sound.

Oh, man, she was hurting bad, for sure. She blinked, the tears pouring down her cheeks.

Pulling herself together again, Angie screamed angrily, and tried to fight back. Flailing with both hands. But he allowed her little room to maneuver, crowding in even closer now with his massive upper body, and crushing her almost flat against the pickup's door. She couldn't move now, felt trapped.

He drew back suddenly and was pounding her with her own pencil… heavy-handed, thudding, sharp blows stabbing her painfully in her arms, hands, neck and chest—

She was trying to holler out for assistance now, "No, no, no! Help, help!"

It was a useless effort, obviously nobody else around to hear her cries.

Then he stabbed her squarely in the throat, almost a paralyzing blow. "Shut the fuck up, bitch!"

Stunned, Angie began coughing after swallowing a mouthful of her own blood, then choking and gagging on the sharp, metallic taste… Almost retching up.

But the big guy only stabbed her again, her lower chest making a funny wheezing sound now, like a big balloon slowly loosing air.

And he continued to pummel her, grunting and swearing, stabbing, stabbing, and stabbing.

By now the cab of the pickup seemed to be far away and unreal to Angie, as if this were all happening to someone else, a stranger; almost like she were looking into the truck from outside, and watching a dumb splatter flick…

She blinked again, attempting to clear her vision and trying to groan a weak protest, but she managed only a funny gurgling sound… Angie was drifting now, sinking down into freezing water, everything turning real dark as the cold seemed to quickly invade her in its fierce, icy grip, stealing her remaining breath completely away—

Darkness.

2

It'd been three days since Thuy Nguyen's murder out on I-5 and the two detective teams had made little progress despite their diligent efforts of authorized overtime three long days and evenings.

No leads at all from any relatives or friends or colleagues at the victim's MIS work team downtown at State General Services. Thuy seemed to be unanimously well liked, a conscientious single, hard-working mother with no known enemies. She'd been divorced a little over a year, her ex-husband living seven hundred miles away in L.A.

with a solid alibi for the time of her death—he was supervising a swing shift at a UPS parcel loading facility with a slew of witnesses. Other than the typical kooky phone calls, no one else had come forward after the Tuesday media solicitations for witnesses. And nothing really in yet from forensics—no latent print matches—none of the mass of lifted prints really too clear—although they were still awaiting results from the smaller military data base. Nothing yet on the DNA either. The lab was supposedly still running the last of the less sophisticated tests.

Katy felt like they were stuck in thick mud, just spinning their wheels. Everyone working the case was getting short-tempered and frustrated, including Captain Silver; the media was howling for results.

That Friday morning, Katy'd met Johnny at headquarters early again, to do some brainstorming. And she didn't even have her coat off when the phone rang on her desk.

She answered and listened to Patrick McHugh, who was calling on his way out to a reported new homicide victim site.

Looked like their Good Samaritan perp may've struck again last night. Dumping the probable victim's body off on the Old River Road leaving Del Paso Heights in North Sac headed toward Marysville, after leaving the girl's car with its hood up out on I-80. The car was registered to nineteen-year-old Angie Jones—McHugh and Bundy hadn't got there and verified yet that the dumped body was actually Jones. But the M.O. looked familiar. The perp had apparently struck again out on the freeway during last night's prime evening commuter traffic—the CHP coming up on the abandoned car at around 6:00 p.m. So maybe they had a serial killer on their hands now. Katy shook her head. *Just wait until the media gets a hold of this new one,* she thought.

Johnny and Katy drove out to the winding two-laned county road beginning just northwest of McClelland Air Force Base. Bundy and McHugh were already there across the county road, interviewing the two guys who had apparently spotted the body on their way into Sacramento earlier this morning around 6:30 a.m. and stopped to investigate.

The body itself was sprawled alongside their side of the road, easily visible from where Johnny had parked his car on the narrow shoulder—leaving a big space to make sure he didn't drive over any potential evidence, including tire prints.

They got out, waving and indicating to the other two detectives that they were going to begin working the dump scene around the body.

Katy approached the victim cautiously, watching where she stepped, and pulling on a pair of latex gloves. After a careful scan around the victim's body, she kneeled over the young woman, sucking in a settling breath, then, without touching her, Katy concentrated.

"Okay, what's up here, girl," she whispered under her breath as she peered down, taking a quick general check, and, as usual, doing her interior monologue up close and real personal.

Oh, girl, it looks like you put up one hell of a fight, Katy thought, still kneeling over the victim, as Johnny snapped some Polaroids nearby. They always took a few for themselves even though the ME—*Medical Examiner*—folks would arrive soon and take the official shots.

"Look at all these defensive stab wounds," she murmured in a hoarse voice, pointing down at the girl's hands and arms, and glancing back up as Johnny moved closer. "Must be seven or eight of them, at least."

"Yeah, I see them, and I'm going to get some close-up photos," Johnny said, standing squarely over the victim.

Both Bundy and McHugh were still across the road talking to the two witnesses, apparently sheetrock installers from Yuba City—their midnight blue Ford 150 pickup's open driver's door read in block silver lettering:

SUTTER COUNTY DRYWALL,
TAPING, & TEXTURING, INC.
CA License # 11129100

Katy looked back down again and concentrated on the young woman's face, whispering to herself: "What exactly happened here? What did you see during your last few moments alive? What can you tell me?"

She'd struggled for sure, Katy thought, no question about that. The young woman's expression wasn't surprised or terrified like most murder victims, but frowning and more angry-like, as if she'd been determined to protect herself. *Fought to the end.*

Katy carefully dropped her gaze down from the victim's face, pausing to look over the multiple neck and chest stab wounds, then slowly down to her foot—her shoe dangling awry. The body was twisted abnormally, too, lying in an unnatural position on its left side, one leg doubled back underneath her, Katy guessing the perp hadn't actually stabbed her there… No. Probably just dumped her out from his vehicle, where he'd attacked her after stopping here on the shoulder. Tossed her out like a sack of garbage.

Blinking, Katy sighed, stood up, moving away from the body and scanning around carefully—

And stopped. She called Johnny back, who was now taking a Polaroid of tire tracks behind her up on the shoulder just in front of his parked car—possibly from the perp's vehicle. "Come check this out, Johnny."

She pointed into the grass down the side of the shoulder, about five yards away from the body. A pencil, not a common No. 2, but a much thicker, fatter type. Katy thought it was a special pencil used in artwork. The thick pencil was snapped almost in two, the intact point and upper third covered with what appeared to be dried blood. It'd probably been tossed out, maybe along with the body.

Johnny came down, nodded, took a photo, and waited for it to develop. Then, he carefully bagged the pencil without smearing any latent prints, before glancing at Katy. "Murder weapon?"

She nodded absently, thinking that it was an odd weapon for the guy to be carrying. Why not something more efficient, like a bigger, sharper knife? *Yeah, why not,* she thought? Then it suddenly occurred to her that maybe the murder weapon didn't belong to the killer. She nodded slowly to herself. Yeah, *maybe* not. It might just belong to the girl. Something she carried with her for protection. I'm guessing you're an artist or an art student, girl, Katy thought, glancing back up at where the twisted, bloody victim lay nearer the road shoulder.

"Johnny, if she's into art, I bet this art pencil belongs to our victim."

After a pause to reflect, he said, "Yeah, seems like a funny thing for our guy to be carrying as a weapon. He strangled his other victim."

"Maybe she used it for self-defense," Katy added, still looking around in the grass for anything else. "And he took it from her during the attack. Used it to stab her, then broke and tossed it, when he dumped her."

"Makes good sense to me, kiddo."

"If so, she might have stabbed him first… He may have a wound somewhere on him… an arm or hand most likely. His blood could be mixed with hers on that pencil."

"You just might be on to something," Johnny agreed, leading them both back up closer to the dead girl. "And that's why the son-of-a-bitch went nuts," he said, nodding his head, "stabbing hell out of her with that pencil, because she got him first—"

At that moment Johnny spotted the little purse tucked almost out of sight under the victim's twisted leg. He carefully went through the several items inside, gripping the DMV license by holding it on the sides between his gloved thumb and forefinger to avoid smearing any latent prints. "Yep, this is Angie Jones alright, kiddo," he said. "Only nineteen years old… " He paused a second, then added, "Current American River CC student body card in here, too." He looked up at Katy and smiled thinly. "We'll check the school out, see if she was indeed taking any art classes." He glanced back into the tiny purse. "No bills, only a handful of small change. A comb, lipstick, a wadded-up facial tissue, and her cell phone… that's about it."

Katy nodded, not saying anything back to her partner, just staring down again at the young victim, all the terrible multiple wounds. She never got used to brutality like this, even after four-plus years in homicide. And someone so young with all her life ahead of her. Maybe a talented artist. Katy sucked in a deep breath, blinked again, wiped her eyes against her bare wrist, and kneeled to continue with her postmortem interior questioning.

Well, your jeans were only partially unbuttoned, girl, Katy thought. And your panties are still intact. *Not touched?* He probably didn't get a chance to rape you before you died in his vehicle, did he? After a few more thoughtful moments, Katy stood back up and stretched. "Guy is a violent sadist, for sure," she said to Johnny. "But it doesn't look like he's a necrophiliac."

She didn't think so anyhow.

Katy watched as a light gray county car with a flash-bar on its roof pulled up behind Johnny's blue Mustang. He normally opted to drive his own wheels instead of something out of the department vehicle pool—a personal quirk. A man and woman stepped out together. Dressed in white lab coats, with easy-to-read nametags hanging around their necks, and carrying their black handbags, Katy thought that they looked more like a pair of medical doctors rather than younger and more hip techs, like from some TV program. She recognized one of the ME techs.

Suzie Kresby introduced Katy and Johnny to her partner, Hsui-ya Yeoung. "Call him just plain *H*," she added with a smile, "we all do."

"How about checking the potential murder weapon, that pencil, for another blood type, in addition to the victim's. We suspect the pencil actually belonged to her, and she may have stabbed him initially." Johnny handed Yeoung the plastic baggie with the broken, stained sharp pencil, and also the victim's bagged purse. "And you may want to check for vaginal semen even though it appears she wasn't sexually assaulted, okay?"

"Will do," the woman said, nodding and smiling thinly. "Actually S.O.P., you know, along with carefully checking over her clothes and the ground nearby, just in case he masturbated postmortem, which isn't all that unusual in these kinds of cases, and—"

"Sorry, Suzie," Katy said, her red face and sincere smile enhancing the apology. "Wasn't thinking about you guys at the moment. Still concentrating on the poor victim. I realize everyone in your whole department really knows their jobs well."

Suzie nodded and shrugged dismissively, saying, "I understand, no big deal." The two techs opened up their black bags and began their crime scene work.

Katy caught Johnny's attention. "Seen enough, pal?"

He looked around, then nodded. "Harlan and Patrick seem to be wrapping up their long-winded conversation with those sheetrockers, too—bet their both Kings' fans." He knew Katy was well aware that the Sacramento Kings had upset the Lakers in overtime last night in the L.A. Forum.

A few more minutes of searching around the debris alongside the shoulder, then Katy said to Harlan, who had come across the road to the dump site, "It is indeed Angie Jones as you suspected. ME troops have her purse, driver's license, and maybe the murder weapon—a sharpened pencil. We'll check her car at the CHP office, if you want to finish up with the lab troops here. Meet you back at the office in, say, an hour and a half?"

He nodded.

Johnny talked with Patrick McHugh for a moment at the side of the narrow road, bringing him up to speed, too. Then he gestured for Katy to meet him at his Mustang as the two sheetrockers left for work.

They found nothing earth-shaking at the old LeSabre that had been abandoned near the Del Paso Heights exit back on I-80, and had been towed into the CHP impound lot off of I-5 near the Sacramento River. But the techs might come up with something after the car was thoroughly examined by them.

After getting back into the Mustang, both Johnny and Katy sat in place and carefully looked over his Polaroids taken earlier that morning. Sometimes the photos, which were narrowly focused, blocked out background distraction and occasionally revealed something not obvious in person to either of the two detectives. Unfortunately, nothing jumped out and poked either of them in the eye.

MARY LOU DUDDY

CRIME SCENE NOTES

Name: Mary Lou Duddy

Ethnicity/ Gender: Caucasian Female

Age: 43 years old

Family: Widowed, no children

Occupation: Owner of an import children's shop on the K-Street Mall: The Dolly Lama

Trauma: Sexually Assaulted, One Rib Cracked, Strangled, Hyoid Bone Broken

!

Tuesday morning, Jack was stretched out on his raggedy, sagging couch in his apartment in the complex on El Camino Avenue in North Sacramento, drinking a Miller Lite, the noon TV news winding down. They hadn't really said much about his latest prey. Only her name—Mary Lou Duddy—a little about her business downtown, not much else. Except they'd mentioned that authorities were indeed looking for a "serial killer" now—the three recent freeway killings linked. He smiled wryly at that. Actually he saw himself as a predator, the freeways his savannah hunting ground. He was only satisfying a *natural innate need*. He required prey to feed his sexual appetite and frequently. And all hunters were "serial killers," for Christ sake, he thought.

Damn old broad from last night hadn't put up much of a fight though. *Uh-uh.* The rougher the kill, the more Jack enjoyed it now. This one probably figured if she'd just cooperated, he'd've let her go.

"Well, that ain't never going to happen anymore, I bet you on that," Jack said emphatically aloud to himself. No witnesses.

He sat up, crushing the drained can, and frowned.

His painting business was going slow, and Jack hadn't worked on a job in five days. Neither of his last two bids even getting back to him—the customers maybe a little concerned about his weight. They both had looked at him kinda funny when he personally handed them the bids.

Hell, he may look a little sloppy now, but he didn't have much trouble scrambling up and down the ladders and scaffolding, he'd guarantee you on that. Man, going on five days. Too much time on his hands. Maybe he'd give Walter John a call. Sometimes they worked together, when either painter needed help. Yeah, he'd call ole Walt later.

A *knock* at the door.

Oh, no, Jack thought, figuring it had to be the old broad from next door, Sandy.

Sandy was tall, thin, and, man—like the old R & B singer, Bo Diddley, said—*She looked like she'd been whipped wif an ugly stick, Big Time.*

Actually, she was pretty good to Jack, regularly inviting him over to dinner, bringing healthy treats when she made them, and sharing books. She liked true crime stuff, too. In fact, she was the one who explained the technical difference between a mass murderer and a serial killer to him just last week, giving him a Time-Life book on all the major serial killers in the last few years. Very fascinating stuff.

But she was always getting too close, invading his space, flirting, trying to entice Jack into staying over again. He'd tried a couple of times after he'd had a few too many beers, but Sandy was into "gentle, loving sex," and didn't go for any rough stuff—not even an ass slap or two. Man, besides being ugly, she was way too old for him, too— probably even older than that Duddy babe last night. He always kept the lights off when they were in bed—even then he had trouble getting a hard-on. She fought the age thing, using wrinkle cream, and was a real fitness nut, once trying to get him to come to her fitness club, implying he was overweight. He'd been really pissed at the time, indignant. If she didn't like him they way he was, that was too fucking bad. He'd even said something to that effect, and Sandy hadn't mentioned anything about his weight again.

He cracked open the apartment door.

Sure enough, it was Sandy standing there, smelling all fresh and looking clean scrubbed, holding out a book. "Just finished this one, Jack. Figured you'd really like it."

He took the book in hand and read the cover:

In Cold Blood by Truman Capote.

He actually remembered them making this into a TV movie sometime back, but he hadn't seen it.

"Good?" he asked, stepping aside to allow her to come in.

It was about time for a cleanup of the apartment, and ole Sandy was at least good at that—in fact, she cleaned houses for a living. He wouldn't even have to ask; she'd just get busy after she noticed the disorganized state of his apartment and dishes stacked up in the sink since her last visit. He grinned inwardly.

She nodded, smiled gratefully at him, and stepped inside.

2

Earlier that same Tuesday morning, Bundy had called Johnny and

Katy back to the frontage road paralleling the Mary Lou Duddy murder site on I-80 near Orangevale just north of Sacramento.

He led them across the frontage road and down to a big dry culvert, which looked to be temporarily housing someone, though vacant when they got there. There was a laid-out bedroll, some wadded-up fast food wrappers, a bag of empty plastic bottles, a half-full water bottle, and a foot high stack of newspapers, including yesterday's *Bee* on top.

Harlan first indicated this all to Katy and Johnny. Then, he turned back toward the Interstate and pointed up at a spot on the freeway shoulder. "Check out the view from the mouth of this culvert."

Katy followed the line of sight up to the narrow shoulder of I-80 about fifty yards away. He was right, of course, the mouth of this frontage road culvert was almost directly below where Mary Lou Duddy's body was found in the back seat of her stalled Toyota. Whomever was staying here may have seen something important last night.

"The date on that newspaper means *someone* was still sleeping here yesterday anyhow," Harlan Bundy said, with just a trace of uncharacteristic excitement in his voice.

They set up a four-hour stakeout rotation among the two detective teams, beginning that noon with Johnny and Katy up first.

That *someone* came back later that night with a huge plastic trash bag full of aluminum cans stacked in a rusty, beat-up wheelbarrow with a partially flattened tire. Katy and Johnny had just taken over the stakeout again from McHugh and Bundy at 8:00 p.m., and they were both taken by surprise with the culvert's apparent current resident.

The homeless scavenger was a woman, and a fairly young woman—maybe only thirty. But it was hard to tell, because Nance-the-Dance—that's what she told them was her name—wore layered, baggy, unkempt clothes and was an obvious semi-freaked-out drug user. *With probable mental issues, too,* Katy thought.

A skinny, gaunt-faced woman, with shaky movements—almost Parkinson syndrome-like, including flailing hand waving and a constantly shifting wary gaze, as if she half expected to be attacked at any moment. The jerky, out-of-control body, hand, and head movements, and especially the paranoia were classic symptoms of heavy, long-time methamphetamine use.

They finally got her to sit down long enough to talk to them, after they'd agreed to first move inside the mouth of the culvert.

"'Kay, yeah, I live here," she admitted, wiping her nose, then leaning past Johnny and cautiously checking around outside. "Part time, anyhow, when it's not raining. Their nighttime special microwave sensors can't look in here, you see." She gestured at the inside of the concrete pipe, which had been decorated with some odd black and orange childish drawings, illustrated with what appeared to be crayons.

She answered Johnny's question about the strange figures in the drawings. "They're the aliens, man, can't you tell?"

Johnny nodded as if that made perfect sense to him.

Katy offered the skinny speed freak half of an egg salad sandwich she'd brought for herself, expecting the stakeout to last much longer. "Want a Coke too?"

Nance-the-Dance readily accepted both, squirreling the food and drink away in her pack roll that she'd slipped off of the wheelbarrow, which she'd left outside. "Thank ye kindly, lady."

"And you were here all last night?" Johnny asked.

The woman frowned suspiciously. "Why you ask?"

Katy patted one of the woman's grimy hands gently. "We were just wondering if you saw anything strange last night just about dark up there on the freeway? Maybe heard something unusual, too?"

The woman glanced down at Katy's hand, pulled hers away, but smiled thinly. "Strange?" Confused, she shook her head. "Nah, I dint hear nothing weird, just the cars whizzin' by like always, you know… commuter traffic 'bout then."

"Never heard anything other than those cars?" Katy pressed softly. "Maybe like a scream or something?"

The woman quickly shook her head.

Johnny sucked in a deep breath, then coughed, apparently the inside of the culvert's sour smell making him turn away, lean forward, and take a big gulp of fresh air near the mouth of the tunnel.

"Why you asking?"

Johnny turned back, blowing his nose in a hankie, and then said, "A woman was assaulted up there about that time last night—"

"Oh, yeah?… Why do'ncha ask the guy in the pickup?"

"A pickup was stopped up there around dark?" Katy repeated,

slightly elated by the response.

"Yeah, you know a highway man in a pickup," Nance-the-Dance said, with a kind of sly look. "He must've seen something hisself, cuz he sure took off in a big enough hurry, peelin' out."

"How do you know he was a highway man?" Katy asked.

The skinny woman leaned and looked back outside again. Apparently satisfied that no one was sneaking up on them, she squinted at Katy, keeping her head and gaze steady for a moment. "Because he had them highway letters on his truck door," she said, her tone that of an impatient teacher explaining something to a slow student.

"You mean the green and blue CT for CalTrans?" Katy said.

Nance-the-Dance nodded. "You got it, lady."

"Can you describe the highway man?" Johnny asked

She shrugged and said, "Nah, just saw his truck."

Then a moment later, after cocking her head for a second, she reached out and touched Katy's shoulder, and whispered, "Didja hear him out there just now, *didja?*"

"Who?"

"One of them alien motherfuckers," the woman answered in a frightened, subdued voice. Her hands were dancing out of control at that moment. "They're after this." She slipped a raggedy, beat-up little brown teddy bear from her stash. "But I ain't going to ever let them have it. No way, man."

"He's after your bear?" Katy said not unkindly.

The woman nodded, making an indignant face like a little kid, hugging the bear tightly. "It's mine!"

Katy patted her hand again. "Okay, okay," she murmured soothingly.

"Sometimes I can buy them off with a bag of cans left outside, you know. I think they may eat 'em."

Johnny tried to redirect the conversation, but it was clear the paranoid woman didn't want to talk about anything else tonight except her clutched teddy bear. She was obviously worried about the aliens stealing it, period.

"Okay, Nance-the-Dance," Katy said with a stern expression, standing up and pulling back her coat, exposing the 9mm holstered at the rear of her hip. "We'll just chase the aliens off for you. You don't have to leave them your cans tonight. How about that?"

"Oh, thanks, lady, thanks!" Nance-the-Dance said, jumping up and joyfully pumping Katy's hand. But still clutching the bear tightly against her chest.

Outside the culvert, Johnny shouted into the darkness, "Go on now, get away from here, you—you, foul creatures! This is the Sacramento Police Department talking. And we'll be watching for you. Nance-the-Dance is our friend. Find your own cans. Leave her alone. You hear me?"

They heard someone scrambling off into the darkness. Someone who was obviously exploiting the gaunt woman's paranoid delusions.

They walked back to their car parked across the frontage road, near the entrance into a small shopping center.

At the Wednesday morning's 9:00 a.m. meeting, Katy and Johnny, with a suppressed sense of excitement, shared about a CalTrans pickup being spotted leaving the scene around the time of Mary Ann Duddy's murder. "That would explain the other victims apparently not being alarmed by the perp," Katy suggested. "A CalTrans guy would be above suspicion when he came up to you on the freeway, you know."

Bundy got right on it after the meeting, checking to see who was out two nights ago in a State pickup in that general area on I-80. He finally reached the CalTrans District Four Director of Maintenance in Marysville, who said he'd check with the supervisor of the highway's maintenance yard in North Sacramento and get back to Bundy as soon as possible.

GRETA SJORDAHL

CRIME SCENE NOTES

Name: Greta Sjordahl

Ethnicity/ Gender: Caucasian Female

Age: 39 years old

Family: Married, mother of three children—20, 17, and 15 years old

Occupation: Part-time bookkeeper for Weather-Gard Insulation, which her husband owns

Trauma: Sexually Assaulted, Cracked Rib, Strangled, Hyoid Bone Broken

The Friday night following Mary Lou Duddy's Monday night assault and murder, Katy and Johnny were first responders to another apparent victim of The Good Samaritan Rapist, five miles east on Highway 116 headed from Sacramento toward the Sierra foothills gold country.

Greta Sjordahl.

It was the first time the serial killer had struck on a State Highway rather than an Interstate Freeway. But the M.O. was the same. The victim was found raped and strangled, left in the back seat of her car.

Saturday morning at the 9:00 a.m. meeting each of the four homicide detectives brought the team current on their individual efforts investigating The Good Samaritan Rapist cases.

After describing the investigation results Friday night out on 116 on the new homicide, Johnny talked about their brief visit to American River Community College on the previous Tuesday afternoon. Angie Jones and her brother were both students out there, Angie indeed an art major. "Katy had an idea about the murder weapon found in the ditch out on the River Road."

He turned to his partner, and she took over.

"Yeah, well, I thought the weapon the perp killed her with was a special kind of pencil used mostly by artists. I was right, it's used for shading in pencil drawings, portraits and such. Since Angie was an art major at ARCC, we figured the pencil might've belonged to her. And she may've stabbed the perp in self-defense, before he took it away and eventually stabbed her to death with it. We were right, two different blood types on the shading pencil." She slid a copy of the lab report they'd received just yesterday over to the others.

Harlan Bundy followed up with his investigation results on the CalTrans pickup lead from the witness, Nance-the-Dance. "The head maintenance guy got back to me yesterday afternoon. They have *no* record of any of their people being up near Orangevale the afternoon or evening of Mary Lou Duddy's murder. In fact there hadn't been any maintenance work on that stretch of I-80 in the last four weeks. He asked me if we were sure about the vehicle logo. I said yes, we thought so. He then suggested maybe it wasn't an active State pickup. Maybe it was one sold off by them. They'd recently had a big auction of older CalTrans vehicles and equipment in Sacramento about three weeks ago. The individual private buyers were responsible for removal of the CalTrans logo. He'd get me a list to check all the pickups sold at that auction, and who bought them. He thought it might be as many as ten vehicles."

After a brief discussion clarifying several areas requiring follow-up, Patrick McHugh brought them up to date on lab results in the first three murders or lack of results, all in his understated way. "No print matches. Still waiting on something from the military data bank—they're down at the moment, have been for several days. No DNA matches yet, either. Lab still doing at least one more test, before searching for matches."

"Friends, relatives, co-workers?" Captain Silver asked. "No leads from any of the victims' acquaintances?" Long John had been sitting in at the last two 9:00 a.m. round-up meetings, asking an occasional pointed question, but making few comments.

All four detectives shook their heads.

A silent lull.

"Well, we need to get some traction on these related homicides soon, people," Captain Silver said, frowning. "The public is alarmed and, naturally, frightened. And The Chief is taking some heavy political heat. So I've asked for departmental approval for getting help from Vice. You know the potential drill, using some of their experienced female undercover personnel in stalled cars placed on the freeway system around the City to maybe lure in this perp."

"Ah, Captain," Johnny said, making a face. "You know those guys from Vice play too fast and loose, especially with evidence—"

"I know, Detective," Captain Silver said coolly with a slight shrug. "Nevertheless, I'm meeting with Captain Marcos at Vice this coming Monday afternoon to go over the logistics of setting up a sting with all the necessary safeguards for his people. All four of you will be cooperating with Vice, and be positively involved, most likely as backup cover during the sting."

It was obviously a done deal, Katy thought. Who knows, maybe it'd help, the four of them hadn't accomplished do-diddly-squat in almost two weeks. And this guy didn't seem to be slowing down any. In fact, if anything, he seemed to be maintaining a pretty steady production quota, a hit every three or four days.

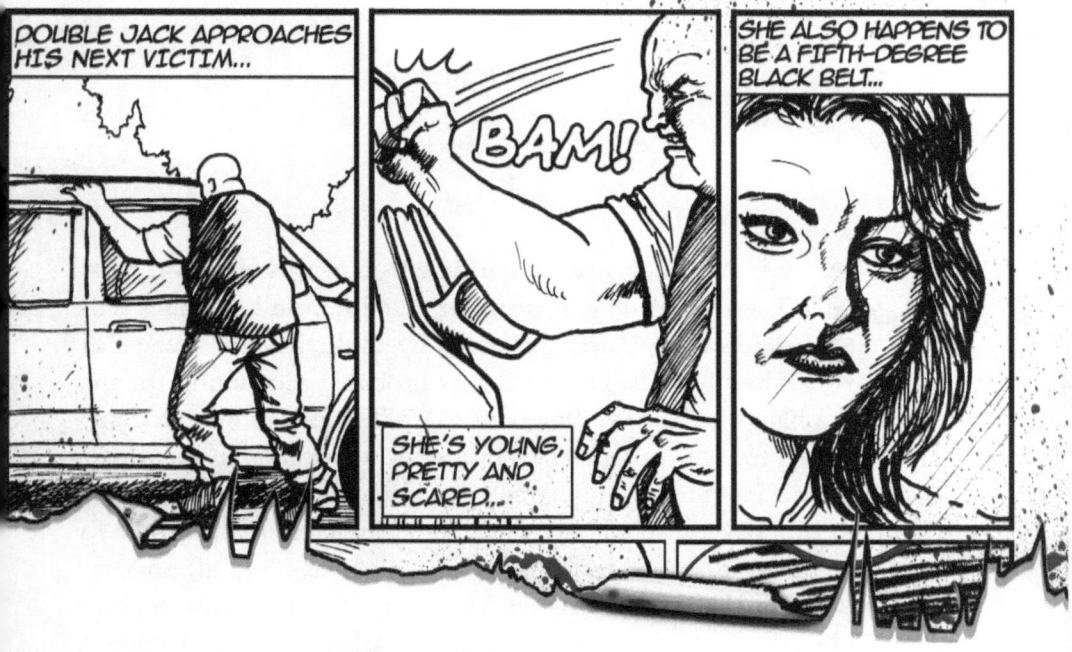

MARIA MARTINEZ

CRIME SCENE NOTES

Name: Maria Martinez

Ethnicity/ Gender: Mexican-American Female

Age: 29 years old

Family: Unmarried

Occupation: Karate Instructor, Red Crane Martial Arts Studio, West Sacramento

Trauma: Minor Facial Bruises

!

Maria Martinez had just finished up with her group early Tuesday evening, instructing an all-female beginning self-defense class. Fear generated by all the media coverage of The Good Samaritan Rapist probably accounting for the almost doubling in class size since last week. The eleven new students ranged in age from a young teenager to a pair of women in their mid-sixties. Maria taught only one other beginning Karate class at Red Crane on Monday and Wednesday evenings, leaving her ample time to train in Okinawan-style Karate during her mornings and afternoons. She was a Chi dan black belt—seventh degree, one of the highest attained by any female in the western states, earlier this year. A current champion in her competitive level and weight class in the region, headed for the national finals in Philadelphia at the end of the year. If she placed well she intended to use the media attention as PR and open her own small dojo studio, perhaps up in Roseville or Auburn.

But right now she was in a hurry to get downtown to her apartment on J Street near Sutter General Hospital and across from Sutter Fort. She had to grab a quick bite to eat, shower, and change before meeting a Southwest flight at Sacramento International Airport coming in at 7:55 p.m. from Seattle. She was picking up Ken-Jo Kendo at his second stop on a West Coast tour—his first stateside visit. Ken-jo-san had been her *Sensei* at the famed Ishikawa Dojo on Okinawa. He would be staying two days with Maria, and she would be driving him to several talks around Sacramento, including a demonstration and discussion tomorrow night out at Red Crane, before he went on to the major stops in San Francisco, L.A., Anaheim, and San Diego in his Okinawan Karate speaking/demonstration tour.

While stationed at Kadena Air Force Base on Okinawa in the late '90s, Maria had become fascinated with Okinawan-style Karate, reenlisting in the Air Force and extending through three more Far Eastern tours in order to continue studying at the famed dojo under the esteemed Ken-jo-san and other Okinawan masters. During that four-and-a-half-year period she'd earned her first five black belts. In addition to dramatically improving her physical martial arts prowess, her study at the dojo had required her to focus on and enhance psychological and spiritual aspects of her life, including deep-level meditation, which she practiced daily. She'd left the States an immature girl seeking direction and purpose, and returned a well-rounded, young woman—thoughtful, poised, and confident. Naturally, she continued to train and compete in Karate after she was eventually discharged from the Air Force at Keesler AFB in Mississippi three years ago, and returned to her hometown of Sacramento.

Maria was honored and indeed excited that her renowned *sensei* had made a special stop in Sacramento for her on his tour, and agreed to a brief demonstration at her school.

She sped her Saturn sedan north along Business I-80 back from West Sac into the City proper, but something happened just before going under the I-5 overpass, the motor cutting out. She glided to a complete stop on the shoulder of the Freeway, the lights from the Capitol building in view directly ahead of her in downtown Sacramento. She tried the starter… Nothing happened, the car not turning over at all.

Now what—?

And that's when the big man appeared like a ghost out of the night at her rolled-up window, startling her. He was gesturing for her to roll down her window.

Maria had an instant bad feeling about this guy coming up on her so suddenly out of the night. Normally, she wasn't easily spooked or overly frightened by anyone she encountered, day or night. But this guy was huge, a moving mountain and scary-appearing despite his wide smile. Uh-uh, she wasn't rolling the window down for him. No way.

Maria shook her head and shouted through the glass at him. "What do you want?"

He rattled her locked door, the big smile disappearing slowly from his face.

Maria was fully alert and wary now. This guy could definitely be that killer from the *Bee* articles. She wasn't taking any chances. She leaned over to get her purse, reaching in it for her cell phone.

But that's when he started to bang heavily on her window with his doubled fist, and he was actually red-faced now, looking pissed. He was swearing, too.

And he was threatening to break her window if necessary to get in…

Time for her to be proactive. Maria stretched out across the passenger seat away from the ranting man banging her car window, tucked up her left leg to her chest—

Then, with a loud *grunt* and a forceful strike into the driver's door handle, she sent the car door flying open and slamming into the man's red face.

She slid out the opened door, assuming an offensive position… But this guy was surprisingly quick, considering his huge size and injured condition—the door had opened a long, deep gash down his cheekbone, and he was bleeding heavily. Nevertheless, with a kind of nimble hop step, he closed in, smothering a hand strike by Maria, while simultaneously attempting to wrap her up in a tight bear hug.

But before he could pull her close enough to adequately lock his grip, Maria deftly sagged her knees slightly while explosively lifting up both hands together and against his underarms, breaking his tentative hold. Following up instantly, she stepped back while leaning slightly to the right, centered herself, and delivered a round-house kick with her left leg, which brushed his shoulder, losing some power, but striking him solidly in his forehead.

The deflected blow didn't even faze the big guy.

He just roared angrily, "You fucking bitch!"

And then he attacked Maria almost like a heavyweight boxer, striking out with two solid left jabs to her face, before following up with a wild, heavy-handed round-house right that luckily sailed over her ducking head.

Skillfully, she shuffled out of his punching range and assumed an attack position, before moving back in and delivering two lightning quick, fully-pronated knuckle strikes that thudded loudly into the big man's throat with enough force to crack his windpipe. She drew back a step ready to follow up with a straight leg kick to the chest.

But the giant slid down on one knee, gasping for breath, but still not out, and he was fumbling with something in his right jacket pocket.

Gun, knife?

It figured this nutcase would probably be armed for his nightly assaults. Before he withdrew a weapon, Maria decided it was time to escape while she still had a good opportunity.

She dashed off, leaving her assailant still down near her car.

A block away she got a motorist to stop; but he didn't have a cell, and they wasted five minutes finding a pay phone off the freeway. They finally got through to the police, but the responding officers were too late to catch her attacker back out on Business I-80 near her disabled car.

2

Jack had taken a shaking blow to his ego. *A fucking five-foot midget,* he thought, *kicking my ass like that? And a woman!*

Unbelievable. But she was using that Kung-Fu shit, man, he reminded himself—as if that explained everything... Still, I'm a little out of shape, he grudgingly admitted to himself, breathing heavily as he sped off toward his apartment in North Sac. Man, I gotta lose some weight, and fast, get my ass back in condition.

In his first tour in the Navy, he'd lifted weights and boxed quite a bit in smokers onboard ship—even kicked some serious ass. He knew he couldn't possibly go even one round now.

First thing on arriving home, Jack rapped on Sandy's apartment door.

She was delighted to see him, but concerned about the wound on his cheek.

He dismissed her concern. "I need that card with your fitness place address," he said, still angered by the night's embarrassing dishing of humility. "Can I maybe go down tonight with you as a guest, work out, and then get myself signed up?"

"You sure can, sweetie," Sandy said, "but I'm getting you a Band-Aid first."

3

After talking with Maria Martinez for only a few seconds down at headquarters, Katy had that special tingling in her stomach—she knew they were going to close in on their guy now. And that's how she'd refer to The Good Samaritan Rapist from then on. Everyone in homicide slipped into using that phrase when they felt they were definitely closing in on a perp: *Our guy* or *Our boy*.

"And you think you could come back early tomorrow morning, accurately describe him, and help a police artist do a likeness?" she asked Maria, who had actually verbally described her attacker in pretty amazing detail. With her martial arts training, she'd remained apparently extremely calm, able to observe even the slightest details, like a dark mole on his left cheek, a tiny white scar in his left eyebrow, the golden-brown color of his eyes, and his short brown ponytail—held in place with a common doubled red rubber band. Of course it was the man's gross heaviness that would be the most telling physical characteristic, Katy thought, after listening as the woman went on for another two minutes, describing other details, even demonstrating how he moved—a shuffling but quick and agile hop and glide—all in very precise language. Yeah, it sounded like the guy was unusually large, at least 6-foot-3-inch, maybe a little taller, and weighing well over 350 pounds. Big dude.

"Yes, I can come back tomorrow morning and help your artist," Maria answered confidently.

Katy and Johnny listened quietly as the young woman then described chronologically in detail what had transpired tonight from the moment she left work, stalled-out around 6:15 p.m. near the Capitol on I-80 Business, and was immediately confronted by The Good Samaritan Rapist. At least Katy figured it had to be their boy—the M.O. fit perfectly.

And throughout her scary encounter, the young woman had only received two minor bruises on her cheek in what was an obvious mismatch. Katy glanced over at her partner. From his expression, Johnny, too, was obviously impressed with Maria's prowess and descriptive ability.

Inwardly, Katy smiled, as they rose up to shake hands with Maria Martinez as she got up to leave headquarters. The young woman had a guest waiting to be picked up out at Sacramento International Airport in Natomas. Maria was only 5-foot-1-inch and couldn't weigh more than 125 pounds sopping wet, Katy thought. Bet *our boy* is more than just a little embarrassed about getting his big, mean, fat ass kicked by such a tiny woman.

Maria would be coming back first thing in the morning at 8:00 a.m. to talk to one of the artists here at headquarters. Johnny and Katy would follow up with anything else she might remember—but she'd been pretty thorough, more so than ninety-nine percent of homicide witnesses. The one thing that bothered Katy though was that Maria had said the guy had been driving a pickup, which she thought was an old Courier. No CT logo either. What happened to the CalTrans truck that had been working so well for our boy with his past four victims? He owned *two* pickups? That seemed a little unlikely... But nothing seemed normal about this huge vicious killer.

Later that evening, getting out of the shower, Katy had one of her legendary bursts of insight about a perp. Naked, she'd grabbed a thin handle of fat on her hip and frowned, while examining herself critically in the mirror. Even though she tried to work out weekly with an old basketball teammate out at American River, she had still managed to put on a pound or two. Too many rushed fast food meals. Not good. Johnny was a little flabby, too, but he'd started working out again, including going up to Folsom Prison and coaching convicts in a boxing program. But maybe they both needed to sign up at one of the local fitness studios, take time to formally lose a little weight, toughen up, really get in top shape—

That's when the light bulb went on over her head.

Oh, yeah!

"Johnny, Johnny," she shouted out from the bathroom, quickly pulling on a pair of jeans and a green and gold Sac State T-shirt. He'd picked up some Nations burgers earlier and come home with her to her townhouse to eat and talk about the case, before heading off later to his place over on 26th and F Streets.

With a concerned expression, he came hustling into the bathroom. He glanced down at the thin roll of skin from her hip she was exposing in her hand, while holding up her T-shirt. "What's wrong?" He said, a little too loudly, staring first at her skin, and then back up into her face, with a puzzled expression.

She grinned back cockily at him in the mirror. "We got our boy," she said, giggling almost out of control.

The next morning, after Maria and the police artist developed a composite drawing of the perp, they began their canvassing of fitness/health studios, working the north-side of Sacramento, Harlan Bundy and Patrick McHugh, who were enthusiastically on-board, working the south-side. Both sets of detectives were armed with a composite drawing of The Good Samaritan Rapist—a drawing they decided not to share with the media just yet. Earlier Katy had explained about their boy being grossly overweight, and probably deeply embarrassed about getting his ass kicked so easily by Maria Martinez. So naturally she figured he would be enrolled in a weight loss and fitness program somewhere in the City—probably on a crash course, too.

Wednesday afternoon, Katy and Johnny had a positive hit on the fifteenth exercise club they visited. At Fun & Fit, a small club out on Arden Way, near the State fairgrounds, they showed their composite drawing to the manager. The buff young woman looked up immediately from the drawing.

"Yeah, that looks just like John Malenko. He came in here last night as a guest of Sandy Warner, who's been coming here for… I guess a little over a year now. Looked like he'd had his ass kicked earlier, fresh bandage covering his whole cheek. Signed him up after a strenuous work-out last night. Guy appears real serious to get into shape—he needs it, too. What'd he do?"

They spent long enough to get all the personal information the manager had on John Malenko.

After leaving Fun & Fit, Johnny and Katy headed back downtown to run their various checks on him, including searching for any prior warrants, previous arrests, and even digging up his current DMV info. Katy was curious about his vehicle registrations. *Yes*, he'd bought and registered a pickup from CalTrans only three weeks ago, but also had a '79 Courier currently licensed. Maria had been one hundred percent accurate with her vehicle description. The woman was truly amazing.

That Wednesday night at a late 7:00 p.m. meeting, everyone was excited.

Patrick had come up with a partial military fingerprint match to

John A. Malenko from the evidence gathered at the Thuy Nguyen homicide site. Even Long John was smiling now and referring to him as "Our boy."

Katy and Johnny would check out John Malenko's residence on El Camino first thing tomorrow morning, Bundy and McHugh acting as backup. They'd arrest him, and then bring him in for a serious grilling.

On the way dropping her off at home, Johnny said to Katy, "I can feel it in my gut, kiddo. The ole electricity. We're getting *our boy* tomorrow morning. I know it."

Katy nodded, grinned widely, and slipped out of the Mustang. She shared her partner's tingling feeling.

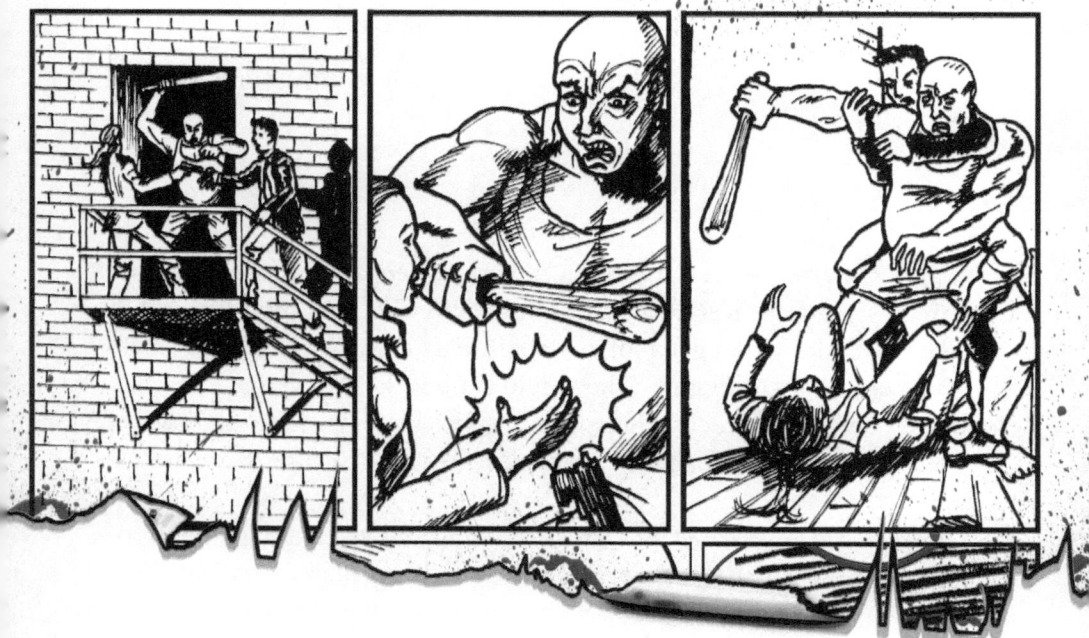

KATY GREEN

Name: Katy Green

Ethnicity/ Gender: Caucasian Female

Age: 33 years old

Family: Unmarried

Occupation: Homicide Detective, Part-time Fiction Writer

Trauma: Broken Right Ulna

!

Early the next morning, they checked around to make sure that Jack's 1979 gray Courier and CalTrans pickups were in the parking lot of his apartment complex, near the 2000-2300 building. They didn't find the CalTrans vehicle—maybe it was parked elsewhere near another building—but the Courier was there between a pair of beat-up wrecks with flat tires. Katy looked about, shaking her head.

Man, this place resembled a junkyard, she thought, knowing some of the run-down apartments were occupied by welfare recipients, the majority of them single mothers, who owned or were making payments on the assorted collection of broken-down junkers in the parking lot. Katy had been in here maybe a half-dozen times four years ago, when she was still working child/spousal abuse before her present homicide assignment. She knew her way around the dilapidated complex of triple-story buildings fairly well. But the place hadn't even been painted since those days years ago.

She first looked over the equipment in the bed of the pickup—he was apparently a painting contractor, working for himself, probably unlicensed. He's lucky none of his stuff was ripped off last night, leaving it out here like that. The good news for them was he wasn't at work this morning. Then, she leaned over and peered into the pickup, wondering how the devil a man Malenko's size got in and out of this smallish cab? In fact, how in the hell did he climb up and down ladders all day painting places? Especially during the summer when Sac got really hot. Then she remembered Maria commenting on Malenko's exceptional agility. She pulled back out of the truck cab, turning to make a comment to her partner—

But Johnny was violently shaking his walky-talky. "Damn it!" he swore, finally holstering the piece of equipment. "You bring your cell?" he asked.

"Left it in the Mustang," she said.

"It's past time the department sprung for cell phones for all of us, regardless their unsecured nature and expense. I think the batteries or something are shot in this damned thing—it was used last in Vietnam, for chrissake!' He took a deep breath, then continued: "Not sure what's going on with our backup. Patrick and Harlan could be anywhere in here. We should've waited and all come along together this morning, instead of just meeting here." He looked around, made a face, and said, "This complex is a friggin' maze, kiddo. We better wait and make sure they're in the right lot, headed for the right building, before we go any farther, you know."

"Uh-uh," Katy said, checking her standard issue .38. "Our boy's most likely home at this early hour. His equipment's in his truck. Let's take him down, *now.*" Her stomach muscles were tightened with the really intense tingling feeling again.

Johnny rubbed his badly broken nose—something he often did when nervous or unsure of himself, tentatively shaking his head. "Ah, Katy, you know the drill. Captain Silver will have our asses sucking buttermilk if anything goes wrong out here, and he finds out we broke procedure by *not* wearing vests; and then, of all things, going ahead before our backup even arrived. Actually not even knowing where our backup *was.*" He shrugged apologetically.

She nodded, smiled sweetly, and said, "Long John doesn't ever have to know, pal. We're going in right now." Then she beckoned him to follow with her drawn weapon.

At the edge of the parking lot, they paused, peering around cautiously, looking for residents, and staring at the stairs leading up to the second level and Jack's apartment, number 2217 in the 2100-2300 building. They saw no one, not even kids, although there were a pair of abandoned Big Wheels, a skateboard, and an old bike lying near the stairway to the second and third levels.

"Where in the hell is everyone?" Johnny whispered, a sharp edge of puzzlement in his tone. "This place is quieter than a graveyard after midnight."

"Too early yet," Katy whispered back, glancing at her watch. It was just 7:05 a.m. "Few mothers work in here, everyone's probably still asleep, including all the kids. And that's good for us. They'll be stirring real soon though to get their kids off to school."

The two homicide detectives left the cover of the dark cluttered parking lot, hurrying to the stairwell, the cemetery-quiet stillness of the big shabby complex slightly unnerving. At the second level, Johnny signaled for Katy to wait a moment, while he leaned out from the shaky railing, surveying the big parking-lot-disguised-as-a-junkyard. He looked back at her, frowned, rubbed his nose, and shrugged. Apparently, still no backup.

She smiled and mouthed: *Oh well*, knowing McHugh and Bundy would be along shortly. They probably were confused by the maze-like spread of the complex of ten or twelve 3-story similar buildings. She and Johnny weren't taking too big of a risk, Katy rationalized silently. She did *not* want to let their boy get away this morning. They'd have to give the media his likeness real soon. Then, who knew what he'd do.

After checking the first apartment door to the left of the stairwell, 2210, Katy signaled for them to turn right, leading the way along the narrow porch, past 2211, easing by two more odd-numbered doors before she paused, pointing at the next apartment, her heart pounding in her chest, her pulse racing. *Jesus*, she thought, taking two long, deep breaths, *I never get used to this shit.*

Johnny bent over and duck-walked, so he wasn't visible from the window of 2217—even though ragged shades were drawn, blocking any casual view in or out—and moved to the far side of the apartment door, Katy staying in place just beyond the door to the adjoining apartment—

Suddenly, the apartment door *behind* her, 2215, jerked open and there was shirtless John Malenko, wearing only a pair of boxer shorts and an angry scowl, his wet hair pulled back in a pony tail, reminding Katy of a sumo wrestler gone berserk, except this sumo wrestler was holding a Louisville Slugger baseball bat instead of a sword, waving it in a threatening manner and quickly moving toward her. The address had been wrong; or maybe he'd been visiting a girlfriend last night; or who knew what—?

"Stop, Police!" Katy said, the command little more than a pair of indistinct croaks.

"Cops," the fat man growled fiercely, spitting the word out as if it tasted bad on his tongue. Then he held the bat tightly in both hands and swung it in a circle, like Mark McGwire in the on-deck circle, but looping it forcefully in the direction of Katy's head.

She frantically jerked off a round from the .38, hitting the big man high in the chest; but, even though he shuddered noticeably, he still managed to follow through strongly and whack her with the bat, the blow glancing off her right arm, which she had instinctively raised to shield her face. Katy was driven back by the terrific force of the blow, almost flipping over the low railing behind her, sharp pain exploding just below the elbow and shooting up her arm. Only by quick reflex she caught her balance in time, but dropped her revolver, clutching her right elbow with her left hand, overcome with pain, knowing the bones in her lower arm must be shattered into a million sharp pieces, each sliver stabbing a nerve.

"*Oooh, Jeee-sus,*" she moaned, her vision tunneling, sour juices flooding her throat and making her wretch with nausea.

Then, through the red veil of pain she saw Johnny solidly punch the wounded man in the face, snatch the bat away, and toss it over the railing—he'd jumped between Malenko and Katy with his weapon still holstered, apparently afraid of shooting her.

Snorting angrily now through his bloody nose like a wounded elephant, the enraged Malenko was more than a match for the much smaller detective. He clutched Johnny before Katy's partner could get his .38 free from his shoulder holster, jerked him completely off his feet, and shook him as if he were little more than a rag doll; then the huge man pulled the detective close, locked an arm around his head in a strangle hold, and squeezed.

Helplessly, Johnny gasped for air, his face turning dark red as he tried to struggle free, his arms pinned against his sides.

Katy fought back her nausea, blinking and searching the deck for her gun, the pain in her arm momentarily forgotten. *This fat-ass nut is strangling my partner!*

My gun, where's my gun?

Aha.

She picked up the .38, in her left hand, trying to hold it steady and draw a bead on the fat man. But her aim was shaky with her off hand. Instead of jerking off a round at a shifting target, she reached out with the revolver and slammed the barrel down hard on the big man's bare foot.

He roared with pain, tumbled over near the railing, but managed to maintain his grip on Johnny, pulling the semi-conscious detective down to the deck alongside him.

Time slowed, Katy's vision again blurring, as she tried to aim the unsteady barrel of the .38 for a clear shot at the giant.

Oh, shit—!

Just as she began to squeeze off a shot, Johnny was jerked around, partially shielding Malenko.

She was forced to ease off on the trigger.

Finally at the last moment, their backup arrived—Harlan Bundy and Patrick McHugh, the two other homicide detectives—thundering up the stairwell; Katy later swore, that moments just before they arrived she heard a cavalry charge bugling in her head, just like an old western movie. The two clubbed the huge John Malenko with their drawn revolvers, until the wounded man finally released the unconscious Johnny, who crumpled up on the deck beside Katy like a discarded rag doll.

Even though they'd caught the culprit, the collar had been a fucked-up fiasco, a close call for both of them.

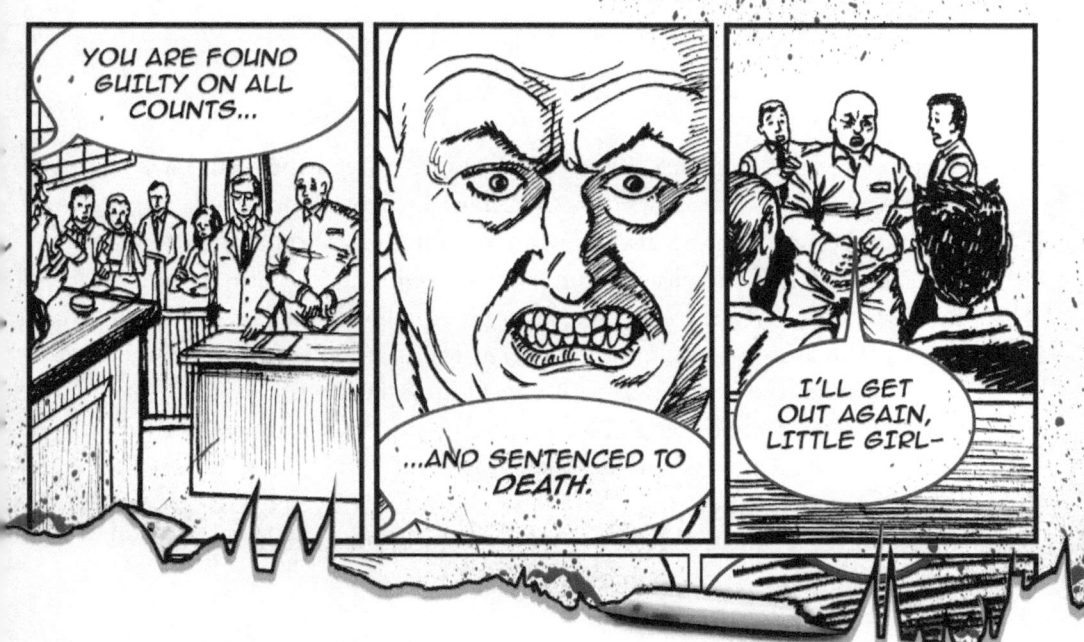

EPILOGUE

K
aty was hospitalized for three days after the arrest, her badly
broken ulna requiring surgery and the insertion of a pin. In
fact, she testified before the preliminary hearing and Grand
Jury with her casted arm in a sling, her partner with
yellowing bruises still on his throat. Malenko himself wore a sling, too.
But she left the courtroom a media heroine, getting credit for figuring
out that anyone the size of Jack Malenko would probably be trying to
control his weight, then searching until she found *his* fitness club.

During the preliminary hearing, after noting his grand size, the
media dropped The Good Samaritan Rapist nickname, and began
referring to the notorious John A. Malenko as *Double Jack*. It fit nicely.

While on worker's comp Katy Green ignored her celebrity status,
refusing invitations to several talk shows including Channel 10's

persistent Serra Melendez of *Saints or Sinners?*. Instead she went back to working on the science fiction novel that she'd been outlining before the case began, and she also went to the range as soon as her casted arm allowed her to grip anything in her right hand, getting Rangemaster Andy Montin to recommend a new sidearm and the appropriate ammo—something with sufficient stopping power to take down a huge, fired-up, sociopath like Double Jack with *one* hit. Andy had suggested a Sig Sauer P-220, a .45 semi-automatic, not really much heavier than Katy's standard issue .38, but with three times the stopping power. They practiced every day with 180 grain JHP rounds until she felt comfortable firing the new sidearm, and in less than a week she was an expert with the more efficient weapon.

Over the objections of his assigned public defender for a delay, Double Jack was brought to a speedy trial only six weeks after his first hearing.

The jury was out less than three hours, returning a Guilty verdict. At the penalty phase trial, John A. Malenko was sentenced to death.

While at the County/City jail in downtown Sacramento awaiting transfer to San Quentin's Death Row, Malenko agreed to an interview with one of the FBI's profilers from Quantico, but only if Katy Green also attended the interview in person.

Katy finally agreed.

Double Jack tried to ask her some personal questions, which she more or less effectively dodged. But at the end of an hour and a half, the notorious killer concluded the interview with something that was vaguely familiar to Katy but still chilling. Something she guessed he'd read and paraphrased from a book—she'd learned that he read a lot, mostly true crime stuff.

Double Jack smiled wryly and declared ominously with a scary frown to Katy: "If I ever get back out again, they ain't going to know where I'm going, but they're going to know where I've *been*... I guarantee you on that, little girl."

The End

... and stay tuned for the next book in the series:
The Crime Files of Katy Green #2: Shadow of the Dark Angel

ALSO FROM DARK MOON BOOKS:

Hearing, sight, touch, smell, and taste: Our impressions of the world are formed by our five senses, and so too are our fears, our imaginations, and our captivation in reading fiction stories that embrace these senses.

Whether hearing the song of infernal caverns, tasting the erotic kiss of treachery, or smelling the lush fragrance of a fiend, enclosed within this anthology are fifteen horror and dark fantasy tales that will quicken the beat of fear, sweeten the flavor of wonder, sharpen the spike of thrills, and otherwise brighten the marvel of storytelling that is found resonant!

Editor Eric J. Guignard and psychologist K. H. Vaughan, PhD also include companion discourse throughout, offering academic and literary insight as well as psychological commentary examining the physiology of our senses, why each of our senses are engaged by dark fiction stories, and how it all inspires writers to continually churn out ideas in uncommon and invigorating ways.

Featuring stunning interior illustrations by Nils Bross, and including fiction short stories by such world-renowned authors as John Farris, Ramsey Campbell, Poppy Z. Brite, Darrell Schweitzer, and Richard Christian Matheson, amongst others.

Intended for readers, writers, and students alike, explore *THE FIVE SENSES OF HORROR*!

Order your copy at www.darkmoonbooks.com or www.amazon.com
ISBN-13: 978-0-9988275-0-6

ALSO FROM DARK MOON BOOKS:

Death. Who has not considered their own mortality and wondered at what awaits, once our frail human shell expires? What occurs after the heart stops beating, after the last breath is drawn, after life as we know it terminates?

Does our spirit remain on Earth while the body rots? Do the remnants of our soul transcend to a celestial Heaven or sink to Hell's torment? Can we choose our own afterlife? Can we die again in the hereafter? Are we given the opportunity to reincarnate and do it all over? Is life merely a cosmic joke or is it an experiment for something greater? Enclosed in this Bram Stoker-award winning anthology are thirty-four all-new dark and speculative fiction stories exploring the possibilities *AFTER DEATH . . .*

Illustrated by Audra Phillips and including stories by: **Steve Rasnic Tem**, **Bentley Little**, **John Langan**, **Simon Clark**, **Lisa Morton**, **Joe McKinney**, **Ray Cluley**, **David Tallerman**, and exceptional others.

"Though the majority of the pieces come from the darker side of the genre, a solid minority are playful, clever, or full of wonder. This strong anthology is sure to make readers contemplative even while it creates nightmares."
—*Publishers Weekly*

"In Eric J. Guignard's latest anthology he gathers some of the biggest and most talented authors on the planet to give us their take on this entertaining and perplexing subject matter . . . highly recommended."
—*Famous Monsters of Filmland*

"An excellent collection of imaginative tales of what waits beyond the veil."
—*Amazing Stories Magazine*

Order your copy at www.darkmoonbooks.com or www.amazon.com
ISBN-13: 978-0-9885569-2-8

ALSO FROM DARK MOON BOOKS:

Darkness exists everywhere, and in no place greater than those where spirits and curses still reside. Tread not lightly on ancient lands that have been discovered by this collection of intrepid authors.

In *DARK TALES OF LOST CIVILIZATIONS*, you will unearth an anthology of twenty-five previously unpublished horror and speculative fiction stories, relating to aspects of civilizations that are crumbling, forgotten, rediscovered, or perhaps merely spoken about in great and fearful whispers.

What is it that lures explorers to distant lands where none have returned? Where is Genghis Khan buried? What happened to Atlantis? Who will displace mankind on Earth? What laments have the Witches of Oz? Answers to these mysteries and other tales are presented within this critically acclaimed anthology.

Including stories by: **Joe R. Lansdale, David Tallerman, Jonathan Vos Post, Jamie Lackey, Aaron J. French**, and twenty exceptional others.

"The stories range from mildly disturbing to downright terrifying . . . Most are written in a conservative, suggestive style, relying on the reader's own imagination to take the plunge from speculation to horror."
—*Monster Librarian Reviews*

"Several of these stories made it on to my best of the year shortlist, and the book itself is now on the best anthologies of the year shortlist."
—*British Fantasy Society*

"Almost any story in this anthology is worth the price of purchase. The entire collection is a delight."
—*Black Gate Magazine*

Order your copy at www.darkmoonbooks.com or www.amazon.com
ISBN-13: 978-0-9834335-9-0

ALSO FROM DARK MOON BOOKS:

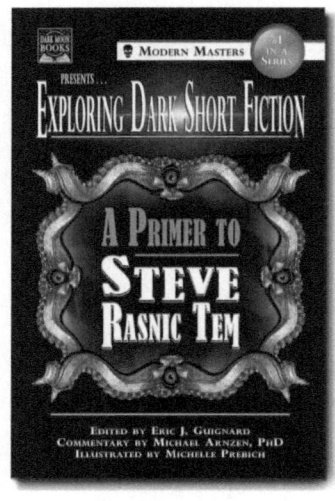

Exploring Dark Short Fiction #1: A Primer to Steve Rasnic Tem

For over four decades, Steve Rasnic Tem has been an acclaimed author of horror, weird, and sentimental fiction. Hailed by *Publishers Weekly* as "A perfect balance between the bizarre and the straight-forward" and *Library Journal* as "One of the most distinctive voices in imaginative literature," Steve Rasnic Tem has been read and cherished the world over for his affecting, genre-crossing tales.

Dark Moon Books and editor Eric J. Guignard bring you this introduction to his work, the first in a series of primers exploring modern masters of literary dark short fiction. Herein is a chance to discover—or learn more of—the rich voice of Steve Rasnic Tem, as beautifully illustrated by artist Michelle Prebich.

Included within these pages are:

- Six short stories, one written exclusively for this book
- Author interview
- Complete bibliography
- Academic commentary by Michael Arnzen, PhD (former humanities chair and professor of the year, Seton Hill University)
- . . . and more!

Enter this doorway to the vast and fantastic: Get to know Steve Rasnic Tem.

COMING SOON FROM DARK MOON BOOKS:

**Exploring Dark Short Fiction #2:
A Primer to Kaaron Warren**

Australian author Kaaron Warren is widely recognized as one of the leading writers today of speculative and dark short fiction. She's published four novels, multiple novellas, and well over one hundred heart-rending tales of horror, science fiction, and beautiful fantasy, and is the first author ever to simultaneously win all three of Australia's top speculative fiction writing awards (Ditmar, Shadows, and Aurealis awards for *The Grief Hole*).

Dark Moon Books and editor Eric J. Guignard bring you this introduction to her work, the second in a series of primers exploring modern masters of literary dark short fiction. Herein is a chance to discover—or learn more of—the distinct voice of Kaaron Warren, as beautifully illustrated by artist Michelle Prebich.

Included within these pages are:

- Six short stories, one written exclusively for this book
- Author interview
- Complete bibliography
- Academic commentary by Michael Arnzen, PhD (former humanities chair and professor of the year, Seton Hill University)
- . . . and more!

Enter this doorway to the vast and fantastic: Get to know Kaaron Warren.

**Order your copy at www.darkmoonbooks.com or www.amazon.com
ISBN-13: 978-0-9989383-0-1**

ALSO FROM GENE O'NEILL AND DARK MOON BOOKS:

SHADOW OF THE DARK ANGEL

—Book #2 in the series, *THE CRIME FILES OF KATY GREEN*

Samuel Kubiak has severe issues. A distraught survivor of the California Foster Care System, he suffers from a condition of alopecia, incessant bullying, and a bizarre sexual frustration... But just as life seems its worst, he's visited by a dark guardian angel: One who whispers into his ear that by walking in His shadow, Samuel can avenge himself on all who have wronged him.

And so do a string of grisly murders begin to emerge across Sacramento, victims whose killer seems to have emerged from nowhere and left without leaving any clue.

Assigned to the gruesome case are homicide detectives Katy Green and Johnny Cato, dubbed by the press as Sacramento's "Green Hornet and Cato." There hasn't been a case yet they haven't solved, but now how can they track down a psychopathic suspect that comes and goes in the shadows?

Discover why readers have been applauding this stark, fast-paced noir series by multiple-award-winning author, Gene O'Neill! Read *SHADOW OF THE DARK ANGEL* and then continue the shocking case files of Sacramento's "Green Hornet and Cato":

- *THE CRIME FILES OF KATY GREEN #1: DOUBLE JACK* (a novella)

- *THE CRIME FILES OF KATY GREEN #3: DEATHFLASH*

Order your copy at www.darkmoonbooks.com or www.amazon.com
ISBN-13: 978-0-9988275-8-2

ALSO FROM GENE O'NEILL AND DARK MOON BOOKS:

DEATHFLASH

—Book #3 in the series, *THE CRIME FILES OF KATY GREEN*

Young Billy Williams has been elevated to status of Shepherd of the Flock—leader of a zealous religious cult—and granted gift of the Deathflash, the ability to see the soul as it departs its mortal form at demise.

Billy is also given an ancient knife-like talon and "commanded to do the Lord's work," which he does fanatically, slaying drug addicts in San Francisco who are poisoning their bodies with heroin...

Retired police detectives Katy Green and Johnny Cato find themselves drawn into the grim case of the murdered underclass, whom no one seems to care about until the brother of a victim comes forward with his incredible suspicions...

So begins a journey of addiction, tracking a killer through the dope dens and seedy rehab houses of the Tenderloin district. But as more time passes, junkies begin to die faster and faster, for Billy Williams has given himself entirely to his own addiction: the rush of viewing the *Deathflash*.

Discover why readers have been applauding this stark, fast-paced noir series by multiple-award-winning author, Gene O'Neill! Read *DEATHFLASH* and then continue the shocking case files of Sacramento's "Green Hornet and Cato":

- *THE CRIME FILES OF KATY GREEN #1: DOUBLE JACK*
  (a novella)

- *THE CRIME FILES OF KATY GREEN #2: SHADOW OF THE DARK ANGEL*

Order your copy at www.darkmoonbooks.com or www.amazon.com
ISBN-13: 978-0-9988275-9-9

ABOUT THE AUTHOR

Gene O'Neill has seen over 175 of his stories and novellas published, several also reprinted in France, Spain, and Russia. Some of these stories have been collected in *Ghost Spirits, Computers & World Machines; The Grand Struggle; In Dark Corners; Dance of the Blue Lady; The Hitchhiking Effect;* and *Lethal Birds*. In addition, he's published six novels.

Gene has been a Bram Stoker Award® finalist twelve times. In 2010 *Taste of Tenderloin* won the

Photograph by Jason V Brock

haunted house for collection, and in 2012 *The Blue Heron* won for Long Fiction. Upcoming in 2017 are the four trade paperback versions of the *Cal Wild Chronicles* from Written Backwords Press, a number of short stories, and a novelette. A long novel, *The White Plague Chronicles,* is a work in progress, parts to an interested publisher.

Gene lives in the Napa Valley with his wife, Kay. He has two grown children, Gavin, who lives in Oakland, and Kaydee who lives in Carlsbad and rides herd on his two grandchildren, Fiona and TJ. When he isn't writing or visiting grandchildren, Gene likes to read good fiction or watch sports—all of them, especially boxing.

www.ingramcontent.com/pod-product-compliance
Lightning Source LLC
Chambersburg PA
CBHW021026120726
47905CB00009B/3197